This book belongs to:

chloe

Contents

Ladybird

Cover illustration by Valeria Petrone

A catalogue record for this book is available
from the British Library

Published by Ladybird Books Ltd
A subsidiary of the Penguin Group
A Pearson Company
© LADYBIRD BOOKS LTD MCMXCVII

LADYBIRD and the device of a Ladybird are trademarks of
Ladybird Books Ltd Loughborough Leicestershire UK

My mum is mad

written by Lorraine Horsley

illustrated by Valeria Petrone

My sister is bossy.

My dog is bad.

My brother is noisy.

My mum is mad.

My granny is wacky.

My grandad is late.

My dad's pushed
the button…

My family is great!

The new babies

written by Shirley Jackson
illustrated by Ann Kronheimer

I went to the house next
door with Dad.

We went to see
the new babies.

I looked in the basket.
I saw two little black noses…

and two little white faces.

I saw two puppies.

Dad said, "Choose one!"

But which one?

I wanted to be

written by Shirley Jackson
illustrated by Julie Anderson

I wanted to be an astronaut.

But Mum said, "No!"

I wanted to be a painter,
but Mum said, "No!"

I wanted to be a doctor,
but Mum said, "No!"

I wanted to be a diver,
but Mum said, "No!"

I wanted to be a gardener,
but Mum said, "No!"

I wanted to be a writer,
and Mum said, "Yes!"

Bouncing basketball

written by Shirley Jackson
illustrated by Jan Smith

I had a bouncing basketball.
I bounced it up and down.

I bounced it through
the house

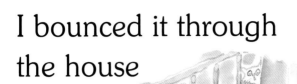

and I bounced it
            through the town.

I bounced the ball quite slowly.

I bounced the ball quite fast.

I bounced it through
        the town again…

and bounced
back home
at last!

Level 1 – Start reading

For a child who is at the first reading stage – whether he or she is at school or about to start school. Uses rhyme and repetitive phrases to build sentences and introduces and emphasises important words relating to everyday childhood experiences.

Level 2 – Improve reading

Building on the reading skills taught at home and in school, this level helps your child to practise the first 100 key words. The stories help develop your child's interest in reading with structured texts while maintaining the fun of learning to read.

Level 3 – Practise reading

At this level, your child is able to practise new-found skills and move from reading out loud to independent silent reading. The longer stories and rhymes develop reading stamina and introduce different styles of writing and a variety of subjects. At the end of this level your child will have read around 1000 different words.

Learning to read with this book

My mum is mad

First, read this rhyming story with your child and talk about what's happening in the pictures. Help him with any words he does not know by talking about the letters and sounds at the beginning, for example, **br** for **br**other, **gr** for **gr**andad, **si** for **si**ster. The rhyme will help him to remember some of the words. This rhyming story also gives practice in adjectives with a **-y** ending (pronounced 'ee'), such as wacky, noisy, bossy.

The new babies

Your child will need to use his wider understanding of how stories work to read this. If he does not recognise a word, ask him to say the letter-sounds. He will also use the context of the story and the pictures to direct him. Encourage your child to go back and re-read the whole sentence that includes the word he has just learnt or corrected. How would he decide which puppy to choose?

I wanted to be

Read the first two pages of the story to your child as this will introduce it. Help him to read the rest to you. Talk about the different occupations explored by the child. What would your child like to be when he grows up?

Bouncing basketball

Read this rhyme to your child and encourage him to read it with you, like a song, before he reads it on his own. Try singing it to the tune of 'I had a little nut tree…' Help him to notice the spelling patterns in the rhyming words:

d͜own   t͜own   f͜ast   l͜ast

Point out the **-ed** ending in 'bounced'.

New words

Encourage your child to use these new words to make up and write his own stories and rhymes.

Go back to look at the stories and wordlists in Level 1 to practise the other words used.

Read with Ladybird...

is specially designed to help your child learn to read. It will complement all the methods used in schools.

Parents took part in extensive research to ensure that **Read with Ladybird** would help your child to:

- take the first steps in reading
- improve early reading progress
- gain confidence in new-found abilities.

The research highlighted that the most important qualities in helping children to read were that:

- books should be fun – children have enough 'hard work' at school
- books should be colourful and exciting
- stories should be up to date and about everyday experiences
- repetition and rhyme are especially important in boosting a child's reading ability.

The stories and rhymes introduce the 100 words most frequently used in reading and writing.

These 100 key words actually make up half the words we use in speech and reading.

The three levels of **Read with Ladybird** consist of 22 books, taking your child from two words per page to 600-word stories.

Read with Ladybird will help your child to master the basic reading skills so vital in everyday life.

Ladybird have successfully published reading schemes and programmes for the last 50 years. Using this experience and the latest research, **Read with Ladybird** has been produced to give all children the head start they deserve.